Copyright and Disclaimer
Woofy Woo Woo the Artist Dog
Written by Louise Elisabeth Robertson

Copyright © 2017 Louise Robertson Emmett
Edited by: DogEarPublishing
Graphic design by: Katherine Varga,
rinvarga@gmail.com

ISBN 978-1-4575-5782-8

TalesILove.com
2017
First Edition

Woofy Woo Woo

& the

Grand Exhibition

Tales of Woofy Woo Woo ©

Written by
Louise Elisabeth Robertson

Illustrated by Katherine Varga

Thanks, love, and understanding
to my husband Frank and to Rin's parents,
Sharon and Alan Varga.

And also to the 'Real Woofy'--Oscar Woofy Woo

Woofy Woo Woo was an artist dog. His artist family was Eileen the Painter and Malcolm the Graphic Designer. They all lived in a rambling Victorian house in London.

Eileen wore black clothes and floaty multicoloured scarves.

Malcolm wore creams and browns and was always neat and tidy.

It was always interesting in Woofy's house, many artists would come and visit. Woofy had his favourites, he liked Mr Chris, he always came with Black Dog and that would mean Woofy got the chance to play ; there was also Mr David with his flat cap and dachshund.

3

Woofy's greatest favourite was Grantly (he didn't ever bring a dog). When Grantly came to visit, Eileen would get out the French Fancies . Grantly would secretly feed them to Woofy under the table. Woofy found this really yummy even though he knew it was slightly naughty .

Malcolm and Eileen were always busy creating wonderful pieces of art. This particular week the house was absolutely chaotic as Eileen was preparing for an art show.

There were mountains of paintings and drawings in boxes and folders all stacked
up by the front door waiting to be delivered to the gallery. There were so many
boxes that it was almost impossible for Malcom and Woofy to get past to go for
their walks.

6

That evening Eileen, Malcolm and Woofy were sitting in front of the fire relaxing and chatting. Eileen was talking enthusiastically about the busy time ahead getting ready for the Grand Exhibition Summer Show.

Eileen said that "this was the chance for absolutely any artist in the whole wide world to enter a painting for the exhibition" ... And ...."it's a wonderful opportunity for the talent of young and old to exhibit at the Academy "

Woofy so wanted to be part of the Grand Exhibition Summer Show as he was an artist himself now, if you didn't know!

8

One Tuesday morning Woofy Woo Woo sat at the front window watching the grey clouds dance like silky ribbons in the sky. Everyone was busy, Eileen was rushing around in her printers apron and Malcolm was making some more straight lined drawings in his office.

9

Suddenly a London black cab pulled up outside the house, out of the cab came Woofy's friend Grantly. Grantly was sometimes flamboyant and sometimes not, by that I mean sometimes he wore really fancy clothes and sometimes plain ones instead. Today was a flamboyant day for Grantly and he had taken to wearing a beautifully flowing multi coloured coat.

Grantly's coat was made of all the colours you could imagine, it made him look as though he was floating towards the house. Woofy really marvelled at the amazing picture of Grantly in his coat .The coat was made up of eye catching colours , emeralds, turquoise, violets, magentas, yellows and golds it was such a marvellous and magnificent sight to be seen.

10

The door bell rang and Eileen dropped everything and bustled to the front door ,
wiping her painty hands on her apron as she went.

As she opened the door she flung her arms open wide to give Grantly an enormous hug . Woofy ran to the door too he really loved the look of that coat and he didn't want to miss out if that meant Eileen was getting out the cake.

Grantly seemed in quite a hurry and apologised for not being able to stay for a cup of tea and a French Fancy. The reason for the hurry up was that he had been asked to be a selector for the Grand Exhibition Summer Show. That meant he was able to choose which paintings would go into the summer show .

Eileen congratulated Grantly on his success and gave him another enormous hug at the same time calling Malcolm so that he could come and hear Grantly's fabulous news. Woofy could hear Eileen say things like ..." that's tremendous" and " what an honour. "

Woofy had always wanted to enter the Grand Exhibition Summer Show . He was an artist but also a dog and how can a dog enter such a competition ? Besides he didn't even own a bank account to pay the entry fee! and that would be just plain ludicrous!

Malcolm and Eileen always appreciated Woofy's art and ever since Woofy had discovered paw printing they had given him his own corner of the art studio so that he could make his designs. Eileen and Malcolm had even made a special paw printing portfolio box for his paintings and it sat beside Woofy's bed .

Meanwhile, during all this excitement Woofy had been listening intently and suddenly he saw his chance.

He scampered off to the paw printing portfolio box and chose a small paw prin painting, small enough for him to carry ir his mouth.

Woofy then scampered back to the kitchen where all the hugs and congratulations were just finishing . Woofy crept in unnoticed and hid himself under Grantly's exquisite multicoloured coat and waited .

It was soon time for Grantly to leave and that meant Woofy was leaving too!

Grantly said that he would pop by at lunch time to tell Eileen and Malcolm all about the selection of the paintings. Eileen said "great!"

17   and she would have tea and French Fancies ready for him when he came back.

The black cab had been waiting outside and Grantly again floated down the garden path but this time with Woofy Woo Woo hidden in the sumptuous folds of his coat . Both of them got into the cab and headed off to the Academy. Neither Malcolm or Eileen or even Grantly , had noticed Woofy Woo Woo had left the building!

The journey for Woofy was a bit bouncy and dark underneath that coat. It was also a bit tricky hanging onto his painting as he didn't want to leave teeth marks on the paper.

Soon Grantly and Woofy arrived at the back door of the Academy. Inside Grantly headed at once to the selection room and met some other Artists who were ready to chose works of Art for the Grand Exhibition Summer Show. The selectors all stood around looking at the paintings, prints and sculptures.

The students from the Academy were there help, their job was to help bring in works of for the selectors to look at . The paintings, drawings, photographs , models and sculptures were all different shapes and siz The selectors were very serious when they looked at the Art work and said things like . interesting use of colour " and " this one is inspirational".

Woofy Woo Woo watched what was going on for a while. He could see the art store where the students went to collect the pieces of art to show to the selectors . Woofy needed to get his painting into that room.

Suddenly he saw his opportunity, just as everyone decided to take a break. The students relaxed on two big sofas, plugged in their ear phones and started to listen to their music. The selectors went over to a table where there was tea, coffee and Victoria sponge cake, they huddled around talking enthusiastically about all the wonderful works of art.

Woofy took his chance and doggy commando style crept across the floor to the art store. There he carefully placed his painting into one of the piles, then quickly he scampered back and hid under Grantly's coat without anyone noticing.

The selectors finished choosing the art for the morning and as promised Grantly headed back to Eileen's house. Woofy Woo Woo was really please as this meant he would be back in time for his lunch and his afternoon walk with Malcolm . Oh what a morning it had been for Woofy !

At the weekend Eileen went off to meet Mr Brown the President of the Academy to check over how all the paintings looked at the exhibition. Eileen was really excited to see which art work had been chosen. Eileen and Mr Brown wandered through the gallery looking at the art that had been displayed. They reached Eileen's favourite room, it was full of smaller works of art covering the whole wall from top to bottom.

Suddenly Eileen stopped in her tracks when she saw a paw print firework picture that she recognised, she also recognised the artists signature W.W.W. and she knew exactly whose painting that was, do you?

Eileen exclaimed aloud " How on earth did that get there "!

Mr Brown agreed and said something like ...yes he too loved that fabulous Firework Painting , in fact all the selectors had . However there had been a problem as they could not find an entry number or who it belonged to ! Luckily as there was room and everyone loved it so much they had squeezed it in anyway .

25

Eileen explained that she knew who had painted that piece and she could prove it, she also added how terribly sorry she was and the trouble that this was going to cause. Mr Brown did not know what she was going on about but it was too late as Eileen had dashed off to telephone Malcolm.

Woofy and Malcolm arrived at the Academy (the front door this time), where they were met at the door by a very smartly dressed security man wearing a crisp blue shirt. Eileen, Mr Brown, and Malcolm went into Mr Brown's office while the security man and Woofy Woo Woo waited outside . Woofy knew he was in trouble...

Eileen, Malcolm and Mr Brown came out of the office and surprisingly they were
all wearing huge smiles . As it turned out all the selectors and Mr Brown had
loved Woofy's painting, normally they would not allow an animal to exhibit in the
Grand Exhibition Summer Show, especially as it seemed that elephants all over
the world were now painting pictures.

28

However, it was clear that Woofy Woo Woo had been thinking carefully about the painting and how he was going to show off the wonderful colours and action of the shooting fireworks . So it was agreed that Woofy Woo Woo's painting could remain in the Grand Exhibition Summer Show.

Woofy Woo Woo was even invited to the Grand Opening of the Grand Exhibition Summer Show. It was attended by all kinds of important people wearing bow ties and other fancy outfits. Eileen had been chatting to Grantly and had arranged for Grantly and Woofy Woo Woo to wear matching multi coloured paw print coats for the occasion and everyone thought they looked fantastic.

Woofy Woo Woo was not only an artist dog but an exhibitor in the Grand Exhibition.

Louise E Robertson (FRSA,MSc, B'Ed,PGC)

Louise is a Fellow of the Royal Society of Arts and a Member of The Society of Authors in the UK. Born in Northamptonshire UK. Louise is a successful educator, and has been a Head Teacher in three schools. As a leader of leadership teams in schools in England, Scotland and Indonesia, she has always loved books for children. Louise currently lives between the UK & USA and is now writing for children. She is married to Frank and between them they have 6 children. Louise won the International Book Award for Woofy Woo Woo the Artist Dog in 2017.

Louise would like to give special thanks to Katherine Varga for all her hard work on this book. This is her first book as an illustrator, predeced by graphic design work on other Tales I Love titles, The Naperville Nodders and Mantilla Loses It!

Katherine (known as Rin) is a recent graduate of North Central College in Naperville, IL with a Bachelor of Fine Arts degree in studio art specializing in illustration.

Rin has worked as an intern on the design of two books for their production. She has taken her recently developed technical skills and helped to produce the books for print. This has enabled Rin to also plan and direct her career. She is now working as a freelance illustrator and finds inspiration for Woofy from her own dog who posesses strong traits of schnauzer, Tessie.

Other titles by Tales I Love:

Woofy Woo Woo the Artist Dog

GoGo Bananas

Mantilla Loses It (Ant Antics)

The Naperville Nodders

CPSIA information can be obtained
at www.ICGtesting.com
Printed in the USA
LVOW05s0324251017
553644LV00017B/130/P